Little
Look and Find®

Search with Skye!

we make books come alive™

 pi kids **Phoenix International Publications, Inc.**

Chicago • London • New York • Hamburg • Mexico City • Paris • Sydney

Meet Skye, PAW Patrol's pilot! She is a daredevil cockapoo who flies through the sky!

Can you find her and these other aerial items?

kite

Ace Sorensen

this cloud

eagle

hot air balloon

Skye

Skye flies over Adventure Bay to look for some farm friends who have roamed away from the sleepover.

Can you help her find them?

this cow

this sheep

this pig

this duck

this goat

this sheep

Uh oh! Two polar bear babies have drifted away on the ice.

Help Skye and Everest find them and these other friends:

Mama polar bear

Ryder

Jake

this baby polar bear

Cap'n Turbot

this baby polar bear

The pups and the Kitty Catastrophe Crew are earning their yellow belts!

Can you find these karate-chopping kitties as the PAW Patrol pups patiently wait their turns?

When the Kitty Catastrophe Crew swipes the carnival prizes, Skye takes to the sky to find them!

Can you find these colorful bunny toys?

pink

purple

green

orange

yellow

blue

The PAW Patrol has fixed the barn—just in time for Farmer Al and Farmer Yumi's wedding!

Can you find these wonderful wedding things?

this bouquet

this gift

cake

disco ball

corn decoration

this gift

What's Different?

Skye soars into high gear to get the party started! Can you spot **10** differences between these two pictures?

Up High with Skye

Flutter back to Skye and find these beautiful butterflies:

Everest Hide-and-Seek

No two are alike, but all six are hidden in the scene! Drift back to the snowy game and find these frosty flakes:

Sleepover Search

Roam *baaack* to the runaway farm friends and spot these:

Polar Bear Rescue

When there's a problem, does Everest give up? *Snow way!* Bobsled back to the icy scene and find these tools:

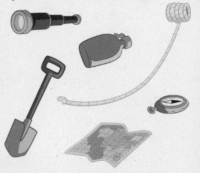

Cat-jitsu!

These pups are kickin' it old school with Farmer Yumi's ancient Pup-Fu scroll! Chop back to the yellow belt challenge and find these things:

Kitty Carnival

Step right up and head back to the carnival to find these festive folks and fairground things:

Wedding Party

It's time to hit the dance floor–they're playing the Puppy Dance! Walk down the aisle to Farmer Al and Farmer Yumi's wedding, and find these rhyming pairs:

Skye • pie
Rubble • bubble
Chase • vase
Ryder • cider
Rocky • teriyaki
Cap'n Turbot • sherbet

Bonus Challenge

Skye makes a PAWsome impression wherever she goes! Soar back over the pages of this book and find 30 of Skye's paw prints hidden throughout!